S0-DQV-078

UPSIDE DOWN DAY

arf.

by MIKE THALER

Illustrated by JARED LEE

A Snuggle & Read Story Book

AN AVON **C** CAMELOT BOOK

If you purchased this book without a cover, you should be aware that this book is stolen property. It was reported as "unsold and destroyed" to the publisher, and neither the author nor the publisher has received any payment for this "stripped book."

To Milt and Mitzi
And All My New Family

AVON BOOKS
A division of
The Hearst Corporation
1350 Avenue of the Americas
New York, NY 10019

Copyright © 1986 by Mike Thaler
Illustrations copyright © 1986 by Jared Lee
Published by arrangement with the author
Library of Congress Catalog Card Number: 86-10872
ISBN: 0-380-89999-X

All rights reserved, which includes the right to reproduce this book or portions thereof in any form whatsoever except as provided by the U.S. Copyright Law. For information address Curtis Brown Ltd., 10 Astor Place, New York, New York 10003.

First Camelot Printing: December 1986

CAMELOT TRADEMARK REG. U.S. PAT. OFF. AND IN OTHER COUNTRIES, MARCA REGISTRADA, HECHO EN U.S.A.

Printed in the U.S.A.

BAN   10 9 8 7 6 5 4 3

Avon Books are available at special quantity discounts for bulk purchases for sales promotions, premiums, fund raising or educational use. Special books, or book excerpts, can also be created to fit specific needs.

For details write or telephone the office of the Director of Special Markets, Avon Books, Dept. FP, 1350 Avenue of the Americas, New York, New York 10019, 1-800-238-0658.

Sylvester Noodle was a down-to-earth kid.
But one morning when he woke up,
something was weird.
He looked at the ceiling.
Something was wrong.

He climbed down from bed.
He was standing on the ceiling.
Something was wrong.

He stepped into the bathroom.
The sink was above him.
He could reach it and his toothbrush,
so he turned on the faucet
and brushed his teeth.

He went back into his bedroom.
He stood on the chair
and opened a dresser drawer.
All his socks rained down.

He opened another drawer.
All his shirts rained down.
Then his pants rained down.
Then his underpants.
So he got dressed.

His mother opened his bedroom door.
"Breakfast is ready," she said.
"Please try and be a little neater."
She headed back to the kitchen.

**Sylvester went to his door
and looked out.**

The whole *house* was upside down!

Sylvester made his way to the kitchen.

"Why are you on the ceiling?"
asked his mother.
"Sit down at the table and have breakfast."

Sylvester did.
He poured out some cereal.
But it all floated to the ceiling.
Then he poured some milk.

It splashed all over.
"Try and be a little neater,"
said his mother
as the toast popped down.
"I'm not very hungry," said Sylvester,
getting back on the ceiling.

"I have an upset stomach."
"No wonder," said his mother,
handing him his lunch box and cap.
"Hurry, it's 7:45."
Sylvester put on his cap.

**He opened the back door
and peeked out.**

The whole *world* was upside down!

He jumped out to the mailbox
and hung there.
"Have a good day," said his mother
as she blew him a kiss and closed the door.

"Good morning,"
said Mr. Jones the mailman
as all the mail fell into the sky.

"Now that's really airmail," said Sylvester
as he watched it all disappear
beyond the clouds.
"Ffur, ffur," barked Topsy,
the neighbors' dog.

Luckily the school bus arrived, and Sylvester swung aboard.

But things were weird at school too.

P.S. 18 was P.S. 81.

And STAR was RATS.

And Band was hard.

And recess was impossible.

Sylvester was glad to swing back home at 3:15.

He spent the rest of the afternoon
fishing for clouds
with his kite.

And seeing how far he could spit.

**After dinner he climbed right into bed
and hoped that tomorrow
the world would turn *right side up*.**

And in the middle of the night it did!

And the next day
everything was back
to normal.